The Dog Who Lost His Bark

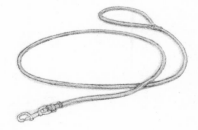

EOIN COLFER

The Dog Who Lost His Bark

ILLUSTRATED BY P.J. LYNCH

WALKER
BOOKS

First published 2018 by Walker Books Ltd
87 Vauxhall Walk, London SE11 5HJ

2 4 6 8 10 9 7 5 3 1

Text © 2018 Eoin Colfer
Illustrations © 2018 P.J. Lynch

The right of Eoin Colfer and P.J. Lynch to be identified as author and illustrator respectively
of this work has been asserted by them in accordance with the
Copyright, Designs and Patents Act 1988

This book has been typeset in Bembo, Ubuntu,
Rosewood, Open Sans, PT Serif

Printed and bound by CPI Group (UK) Ltd, Croydon CR0 4YY

British Library Cataloguing in Publication Data:
a catalogue record for this book is available from the British Library

ISBN 978-1-4063-7757-6

www.walker.co.uk

For Aimee, Ciarán, Aoibhe, Claire and Seán,
the dog-loving Toners of Kilmuckridge
E.C.

For Ken, Danann and Genevieve
P.J.L.

Chapter One

The LOUD MAN called him DOG.

Or PUP.

Or MONGREL.

But mostly Dog.

Whenever he heard the loud man's boots plodding downstairs, or smelled his sour smell, Dog hid far from the door, inside the pile of wriggling fur that was his brothers and sisters. Behind the nippers and scratchers. Underneath furry bellies and wagging tails.

But not near BITER. Biter loved to BITE, and not just

playful nips like the other little ones but BIG CHOMPS that made Dog YIP and WHINE. This was not AWESOME at all. Sometimes MOTHER lifted Biter gently in her jaws and moved him away from the others for being NOT AWESOME. But Biter never stayed away for long.

Dog found a way to deal with the problem. If Biter came close, he would stick his snout in his brother's ear and bark: *YIP! YIP! YIP!*

Three barks. The noise inside Biter's ear made him DIZZY and he would run in circles for a while then fall asleep.

Mother licked Dog when he discovered this trick, and this was EXCELLENT.

PEOPLE came through the door to see the puppies. They brought OUTSIDE smells INSIDE on their shoes and clothes. Dog's mother explained the smells with licks, barks and growls.

This smell was GRASS.

That smell was RAIN.

And when the people from outside pointed at one of Dog's brothers or sisters, that puppy would be lifted out of the BASKET by the loud man. The people would give the loud man some CRACKLING PAPER and then the puppy would go away with them and never come back. This made Dog sad because he did not want to leave his mother like they had, so he hid behind her when people came.

Dog's mother sniffed him and knew by his scent that he was SAD. She told him not to be sad.

Don't worry, she said. *Someday your BOY or GIRL will come. A human who is right for you. And that human*

*will take you to the wonderful OUTSIDE. That is the best
thing for a dog.*

Dog did not stop being sad entirely, because no matter
how perfect his human was, he would still miss his mother.
But now he was hopeful, too. So he stopped hiding behind
his mother when people came. If she said there was a human
who was right for him, then there must be. And that boy or
girl would bring him OUTSIDE.

Later, Dog was taken outside, but only to the yard while
the loud man cleaned the room with his mops and brushes.
The yard was covered in flat stone with only a little grass
poking through the cracks. There had been a flower in a
pot, too, but Biter ate it. Dog longed for the real AWESOME
OUTSIDE beyond the yard, and even though he was still a
little afraid of people, he knew they would take him there
– so he stopped rolling himself into a ball when they came
to look in the basket.

Soon there were only two pups left with Mother: Biter

and Dog. Some of the small people had pointed at Biter,
but he always tried to bite them and they didn't know the
AWESOME TRICK, so Biter
was dropped back
into the basket.

One morning when the bright SUN was in the window, two people came to see the puppies. A man person and a lady person. The lady pointed to Dog.

Dog smelled the loud man's hand coming and he was AFRAID. But the loud man was PRETENDING to be nice with other people there.

Pretending smelled like the BURNED FOOD that the loud man sometimes scraped into their food bowls. The loud man lifted Dog gently out of the basket and handed him to the lady person.

The lady person smelled like FLOWERS and not burning food and Dog hoped that everything would be AWESOME if he went away with these people.

The puppy soon found out that everything would not be AWESOME.

It would be BAD.

Chapter Two

The lady person put Dog in a DARK BOX with some holes in the side and straw for him to sleep on. But the box was so tiny that even a small pup could not stretch out his paws.

NOT AWESOME, thought Dog. But he forgot this when the box was carried UPSTAIRS, and OUTSIDE he smelled the WHOLE WORLD.

Oh, the SMELLS.

Smells to wrinkle his nose and make him cough.

Smells so strong that Dog could taste them on his tongue.

Dog was so excited that he BARKED and BARKED until the man person SLAPPED the box with his hand, which made Dog's head ring.

He stopped barking.

They went on a journey in the belly of a machine that RUMBLED and SHOOK, and this was a new thing so Dog couldn't tell whether or not it was AWESOME. The machine journey ended with some CLICKING and then a SQUEAK.

Dog thought that maybe now the people would let him OUTSIDE in the world, where he could feel many new feelings under his paws and chase things that were TRICKY and FAST. Dog did not know exactly what the tricky and fast things were, but he felt they were out there and he was supposed to catch them. But the people did not let him out. Instead, they left him in his box inside the machine, which puffed then went slowly to sleep, leaving Dog cold and hungry.

Cold, hungry and sleepy.

When the puppy woke up he was in a new inside place. He could smell something which he just knew was a TREE. He had smelled trees before, usually when the smell sneaked in through open doors or on people's hands. But not this one. This one was close by.

A tree inside? thought Dog. His mother had taught him that trees could only be found under the sky and were for peeing on. To have one inside seemed STRANGE but also AWESOME.

Dog was poking his nose through an air hole to get a better sniff when suddenly the inside place EXPLODED into noisy life. Dog heard a loud squealing and the BUMP BUMP BUMP of a young person coming downstairs. When the loud man from before had come downstairs, the bumping had been much slower, but this young person was in a BIG HURRY. The squealing grew louder and louder and Dog was afraid but also EXCITED. The young person did not smell sour. It smelled of milk and warm blankets.

Milk, thought Dog, remembering how hungry he was, and he barked the word: *MILK, MILK!*

The young person pulled the lid from Dog's box, and the puppy saw a boy with a wide mouth and orange freckles. His hands came down and whisked Dog into the air. The boy swung Dog around and around, laughing all the while. The puppy saw he was in a yellow room with soft chairs and a tree, which was covered in lights and had a star on top. The lights S-T-R-E-T-C-H-E-D as Dog whooshed past. Around the boy stood the bigger people, who were clapping their hands and singing.

Maybe, thought Dog, *maybe this is going to be AWESOME. Maybe this boy is MY boy.* He barked the words: *MY BOY! MY BOY!*

But the smiling boy took no notice. Instead, he put Dog down and made people sounds at him while the big man tied a strap tightly around Dog's neck.

"SIT" was one sound the boy made.

"BEG" was another.

The boy made these sounds again and again. When Dog did nothing but pant, the boy made a longer sound.

"STUPIDDOG" was the sound.

And the smiling boy stopped smiling, and twisted his face in a way that reminded Dog of the loud man.

"STUPIDDOG," said the boy. "STUPIDDOG."

Dog whined a little to show the boy how NOT AWESOME the sound was.

The boy obviously did not get Dog's message because he made the sound again: "STUPIDDOG."

And this time the boy poked Dog's ribs with his finger.

The puppy whined louder. Rib pokes were SORE, and Dog thought, *This is not my boy.*

He tried to escape the boy's poking finger but he was trapped against the back of a chair.

All the people were laughing now. It seemed they enjoyed the boy's game. They laughed even louder when the boy lifted Dog by his tail, and Dog felt as if his tail would tear off. Then he would be a dog with no BALANCE! He would never run fast in the big OUTSIDE or jump up to the SKY.

What could he do?

The poking boy put his face close to Dog's and made the mean sound: "STUPIDDOG!"

Dog saw the boy's ear and remembered his AWESOME TRICK for dealing with Biter. He did not want to use his special trick but he could feel his tail beginning to rip. So Dog shoved his nose into the boy's ear and barked: *YIP! YIP! YIP!*

The first thing that happened was GOOD because the boy let Dog's tail go, but the second thing that happened was BAD.

The boy CRIED and HOWLED louder than Biter ever had. The boy howled and fell over into the tree that was inside. Then the tree fell over and the lights went out, and Dog could hear the boy still howling under the tree that was inside.

The big man made a sound: "OHMYGOD."

And he lifted Dog and threw him into a small loud room with two square MONSTERS that had twinkling eyes and circle mouths that went round and round and round.

◆　◆　◆

Dog stayed in the room for a long time and never even saw the AWESOME OUTSIDE. The people gave him food but Dog knew that it was not GOOD food because often the food made Dog sick, and other days the food was so hard that he had to gnaw it off the bowl with his teeth. Sometimes the lady person gave him good water and other times the water was not clear, but Dog was so thirsty he drank it anyway.

The floor was red and white shiny squares, which were slippery, and whenever the lady person came in she would shout the sound: "STAY! STAY!"

Which Dog learned meant NO MOVING. Which was difficult for a cold puppy on a slippery floor.

If he did move, there was no food. And even though the people hardly ever fed Dog, they fed the square monsters with clothes and blankets every day. When the monsters were finished chewing, they would sleep. But even then Dog was afraid and would sleep as far away from them as he could. He made a space for himself behind the mops and brushes and would peek at the monsters from between the handles.

There was no special corner to do his business, so Dog went on some paper that he found on the floor. He remembered from his time in the basket that people went BERSERK if a dog pooed or peed on the floor. Biter had often peed over the rim of the basket and the loud man would chase him with a mop shouting loud words. Every few days, this man person wrapped up the dirty paper and took it away, so it seemed to Dog that doing his business on the paper was the right thing to do.

Then one morning Dog slipped on the paper and everything went everywhere, even under the door. Dog whined because he knew the people would go berserk. But he could not have guessed how much. The lady and the man both shouted at him when they saw the mess.

"BADSTUPIDDOG!"

Over and over they shouted this sound. Then they shouted at each other. Long sounds. And in between their legs, the boy danced and shouted, "POOPOODOG."

And it was this sound that made the man person hop with RAGE. Dog cowered in his mop fort. Even the loud man had never been this angry. The man person shook his fists at the boy and pointed at everyone. Then he swept aside the mops and brushes, reaching in to grab Dog. He tore up the floor, too, ripping it out from under the sleeping monsters. He rolled it into a tube then yanked Dog up by the collar and stuffed him inside.

The boy said, "BYEBYESTUPIDPOOPOODOG."

Dog never saw him again.

The man drove his rumbling machine far away from the poking boy. It was night-time so Dog couldn't see much through the tunnel of red and white flooring, just orange lights that seemed to float in the sky. The machine stopped in a quiet place that smelled of rotten food and plastic. The man was making ANGRY noises, though there was no person there to understand. He lifted the floor tube out of the machine and rolled it out down a hill onto a patch of grass. Dog fell out, shivering. At last he was OUTSIDE. But it was not AWESOME at all! This was not the way he had dreamed it would be.

The man stood at the top of the hill. "STAY," he said. "QUIET." Then he turned and took his machine away.

And Dog did stay. And he stopped barking. Because barking

meant no food. Barking meant big trouble.

He stayed for a long time. He did not bark.

But there was no food anyway.

Chapter Three

Patrick Coin's grandad always said that Patrick was "a great man for the questions". This was especially true when something was puzzling Patrick, and there was something puzzling him now, as he sat beside his mother in the car on the drive to the city.

"Why are we going to Grandad's for the whole summer?"

His mother jumped a little, which was what she did when she was miles away thinking. "You know why, sweetie. A holiday in the city. We go every year."

"Not for the whole summer."

"Because we were invited? And I'm helping your grandad out with the music lessons. The extra money will come in handy."

Patrick was from a musical family. Mum taught the piano. Grandad was a cello teacher. Patrick played the violin a little, and his dad was a fiddle player in a country-and-western band that travelled all around the world.

"Why isn't Dad coming?"

"You know why, Patrick. Dad is on tour in Australia."

"He was in Australia at Christmas. *And* last summer."

Mum snorted. "Your dad's popular in Australia. *Really* popular."

"After Australia? Will Dad be coming after Australia?"

"I think he has some more gigs booked in for afterwards. There was talk of New Zealand."

"He didn't say anything to me about more gigs."

"Dads don't always tell their sons everything."

"Dad always tells me about his tours!"

"Well, there's a first time for everything."

"So, Dad is not coming to Grandad's at all now for definite? He said he might make it in August."

"I don't think so, Patrick. We're on our own this time. We can do it, can't we?"

"We can, but I don't want to. Can I call Dad?"

"Honey, it's night-time in Australia now. Call him just before bed. And we'll be fine at Grandad's."

Patrick knew they would be fine. Grandad's was his second most favourite place in the world, after home. "But we're a family, aren't we?"

"Grandad's family too."

"I know. But not Level One family. Can't Dad come for even a few days?"

Dad usually organized a project for them both when they spent holidays at Grandad's. Last year they had built a go-kart with working brakes.

Mum sniffed. "Apparently he can't."

Patrick sent his dad a sneaky text: Dad. You're not coming to Grandad's? Call your only son! ☹ ☹ ☹ ☹

Then he got back to the questions. "Why did you say Dad was *really popular* in that way?"

Mum didn't say anything for a moment, then she blurted

out, "I've been thinking. How would you like to have a dog to keep you company over the holidays?"

This stopped Patrick in his tracks.

A dog? He could have a dog?

Patrick had never been allowed a dog, because his dad was allergic to everything. Dogs, of course; also cats, grass, dust, olive trees, orange peel...

"What about fish, Dad?" Patrick had once asked him, during a violin lesson.

"The only kind of scales I like are musical scales," Dad had answered with a laugh. "Now practise yours, please."

Patrick had begged for a dog. He'd promised that he would keep it in the garden shed and wear special playing-with-the-dog clothes, which he would never bring into the house. But the answer was always no.

And now he could have a dog, just like that?

Something was going on here.

"What about Dad's allergies?"

Mum had a question of her own. "Do you want the dog or not?"

Patrick quickly nodded. He knew he was being bought off, but he really wanted that dog.

He would get back to the Dad questions later.

Patrick could have any dog he wanted.

"Any one you choose." That was what his grandad said when he drove them over to his local rescue shelter the next day. "My only condition is that it's smaller than a pony," Grandad added. "Other than that, nothing is too good for my favourite grandchild."

This was Grandad's little joke, as Patrick was his *only* grandchild.

But he could have any dog he wanted! That part wasn't a joke. It was a dream come true. Patrick didn't have any friends in the city, but with his very own dog to play with that wouldn't be a problem.

At the rescue shelter he could have chosen the Boston Terrier with its fighter's jaw, or the Pointer with its pointy face, or the Labrador with its coat like a field of barley, but Patrick studied each dog then passed on to the next cage. He stopped in front of the last cage in the row. Perhaps he stopped there because it was the last cage and he couldn't go any further, or maybe the small dog in the cage called out to him somehow.

When Patrick looked at this dog, he felt that he was a potential soulmate. And the little puppy seemed lonely.

I know the feeling, buddy.

That's not to say Patrick had *no* friends. There was this one special pal back home, Eric, but they wouldn't be hanging out until after the holidays. So the truth was that Patrick had no friends *at the moment.*

The dog saw him looking and curled into a ball, revealing a splash of white on his black fur.

That looks like Australia, thought Patrick, remembering his dad showing the country to him on a map when he did his first tour there. *Oz.* That was how his dad referred to Australia.

"Oz," Patrick said softly to the dog, but the dog did not unroll himself. "What's this one?" he asked Zane, the attendant, who lived two streets away from Grandad and occasionally came over for a game of chess.

"It's a dog!" said Zane. "I'm kidding. This one is what we call a multigrain. He's got so many breeds in him that we can't identify them all. Terrier for sure. Maybe some Poodle, and a dash of Dachshund, if I'm not mistaken."

"I want him," Patrick told his grandad.

"No, no, nooo..." said Zane, trying to steer Patrick away. "You don't want that one. This little guy needs extra attention. He's been through the mill. It will take a lot of one-on-one to bring him out the other side. You're a little young to take that on."

Patrick stayed where he was. "I want him, Grandad. You said I could have any one. And he's a lot smaller than a pony."

"I don't know," said his grandad. "Your mum and I will be working most days. Dogs are a lot of responsibility. Maybe we should listen to Zane. I've known him since he was a puppy himself, and he wouldn't steer us wrong."

"The wise man speaks the truth," laughed Zane. "I am the expert. It's not that I don't like this little pooch – I do – but he's got a way to go before he can trust a human. This poor dog's had a tough time of it. We found him half starved, abandoned on a dump site. I checked his microchip and it turns out I know the dealer who sold him originally. Not exactly a prince, I can tell you. This little guy is so traumatized he's lost his bark."

It was no use. Zane could have talked all day and Patrick

would not have changed his mind. Because he had seen the future, and the future had Oz in it.

"This one," he said, pointing at the puppy. "And his name is Oz."

Zane sighed. "Sorry, neighbour," he said to Patrick's grandad. "He's picked a name already. You're done for." He went off to fetch the paperwork for the puppy.

Grandad smiled. "I guess we are."

He squatted down so his head was level with Patrick's. Grandson and grandfather stared at the forlorn dog in the cage.

"Oz, huh?" said Grandad. "As in Australia?"

"That's right," said Patrick. "I bet Dad will like that name."

"Maybe," said Grandad. "When he stops sneezing."

And so Dog found himself lifted once more from the cage and placed in a travel box.

BAD, he thought. *More BAD PEOPLE.*

And he decided to stay as quiet as he possibly could so that these new people would not punish him for things he did not know were wrong.

Chapter Four

Patrick sat in the back seat of Grandad's car with Oz in his special travel crate beside him. He talked to his new puppy all the way home. "Grandad's house is the noisiest house on the street," he explained. "Especially right now. There's a summer music school on. Five teachers and sometimes as many as twelve students. And Grandad the boss of it all, like a supervillain with a cello."

"Hey," said Grandad. "Cheeky."

"So I know all those screechy instruments might be a bit much for a rescue dog," continued Patrick, "but I'm pretty

sure I can keep you away from most of the noise. We're going to be good friends, Oz. The best."

Dog did not move a muscle in case that move was the wrong move. This boy seemed kind right now, but that was people's CLEVER TRICK, to be happy until it was time to be ANGRY. Dog was not going to fall for that one again.

Patrick carried Oz's box upstairs to his room, which was the quietest place in the house – although nowhere in this house was *really* quiet. All the other rooms rang with the whistle, plink and screech of students battling with their musical instruments, and a lot of the noise travelled up through the ceiling into Patrick's room. Patrick put the doggy crate down in a square of sunlight inside the window and then tugged an envelope from his pocket. Inside was a note from Zane, which he'd written as Grandad was filling out the paperwork for Oz.

He tugged out the sheet of paper and read.

(1) Are you sure about the name Oz, kid? This dog isn't going to be doing any wizardly magic tricks for quite some time.

(2) If you do stick with Oz, then call him Oz at least one hundred times a day so he can get used to it.

(3) Oz needs a safe space to sleep in. His very own spot. Not the travel box and not on lino. Oz hates linoleum for some reason. Won't go near it.

(4) It might take a few days for Oz to eat. Just keep putting out fresh food. It would help if you ate some of the food in front of him so he knows it's safe. Gross, I know, but you wanted this dog.

(5) Also, speaking of gross, Oz is very nervous at the moment so keep plastic bags and disinfectant handy.

(6) VERY IMPORTANT: a dog without a bark is not a happy dog. You need to teach little Oz-man to bark again.

(7) Finally, call me any time 24/7. Zane is always available for Oz because I am in-Zane about dogs. Geddit?

Patrick read the note several times then made a few trips downstairs to the kitchen for rubbish bags and hot dogs.

"OK, fella," he said to the little dog cowering at the back of his crate, shivering with every cymbal crash or trumpet toot from below. "Let's get started on today's one hundred. Come on, Oz. Let's go, Oz. You'd like a hot dog, wouldn't you, Oz?" *Three down*, thought Patrick. *Ninety-seven to go.*

By supper time, Patrick had said Oz's name a hundred times and eaten three hot dogs. The last music student had been picked up, and the patch of sun by the window had moved slowly across the room and then disappeared to be replaced a while later by moonlight.

Patrick kicked off his shoes and checked his phone.

Dad had replied to his Call your only son text with this message: Later, buddy. Rehearsing. Drummer is so bad you wouldn't believe it.

Patrick was too excited about Oz to ask for more info on the drummer.

I finally got the dog! I named him Oz after your tour. He won't eat or even come out of the travel crate. Any advice?

He hadn't expected an immediate reply, but Dad got right back.

Oz? Great name! I'm not much help with dogs, I'm afraid. Atchoo! Send pics.

Patrick took a few shots and sent them off, then went back to his training.

Two hours later he had eaten three more hot dogs, leaving only one for Oz should he ever come out of his crate. Then, stuffed and drowsy, Patrick fell asleep right there on the carpet with the remaining hot dog in his hand.

Dog knew that the human boy was offering him food, but he was sure it was a TRICK. As soon as he took the food, then something BAD would happen. Maybe even SUPER-BAD. Dog wasn't sure what super-bad would be, exactly, but he

was one hundred per cent certain that humans had more bad in them than he had seen. So he did not take the food, even though it smelled SOOOOO DELICIOUS. More delicious than anything Dog had ever smelled. He could imagine GNASHING the food between his teeth and how it would feel when he chewed it. How the taste would EXPLODE in his mouth and make the hole in his tummy go away.

But boys could not be trusted. Yes, they started off all smiley, but before you knew it, out came the POKEY fingers. So Dog stayed as quiet as he could and kept his paws inside the crate.

After a long time, the boy fell asleep. Dog could tell the boy was really asleep because people smell different when they are asleep. Colder.

Dog poked his nose out of the crate and sniffed the air.

The smell flowed in through Dog's nose. It filled him up and made him hungry at the same time and was more powerful than any rope, pulling the puppy out of his crate and towards the food thing. Dog knew that it was MEAT, which made a dog strong. His mother had told him with licks, grunts and snuffles that meat was the BEST THING for dogs.

Dog crept forward, using all his SNEAKY SKILLS, hypnotized by the hot dog, his tongue hanging out, panting softly. He was so hungry that his bones ached. He knew the boy would not wake if there was no sound, and so Dog placed his paws carefully on the floor so that he would not make a single peep of noise. He was glad that Biter was not there, for his brother would surely wake the person and then the BAD THINGS would begin.

The meat was close now and Dog longed to chomp it down. He reached out his tongue for a test and licked the food. It tasted AWESOME, so Dog leaned in and chewed the meat right out of the boy's hand. The meat tasted even better than he had imagined, and Dog felt like he could jump up to the sky if he wanted to. But Dog was not ready for jumping just yet.

The food had another effect on him. There was something he needed to do before sneaking back into his crate. And he remembered from the BAD TIME that people had a MAJOR

PROBLEM when dogs did this thing on the floor. So Dog looked around for somewhere close by to do what needed to be done.

He soon found the perfect place.

Later, Patrick woke, stiff in his muscles from lying on the floor. He stretched from his fingertips to his toenails then remembered the new dog.

"Oz, Oz, Oz," he said, getting a head start on the following day's quota. "Are you still in that box, boy?"

Oz was in the crate fast asleep, and in the pale light of the moon, Patrick could see the shining bald spots on his fur where the poor dog had been mistreated. His heart swelled with sadness and he wondered if maybe he had enough love in him to cover Oz, too.

Then Patrick noticed that his fingers had been slobbered on and that the last hot dog was missing from his hand. Oz must have snuck out while he was asleep.

"I'm getting through to you, aren't I, boy?" he whispered. He texted Dad: Oz ate a hot dog.

Moments later, Dad texted back: Result!

When Patrick went to put on his
trainers the next morning, he realized that
they would also be sharing one of those. Gross.
It was his favourite trainer, too, the left one.

Chapter Five

Patrick knew that he had made a small breakthrough. But he was sure it would take more than a few hot dogs and a trainer potty to make Oz trust a human again.

Luckily, there was magic in the house. And this might just do the trick.

The magic permeated the walls of the house every day except Sunday, when there were no music lessons. Patrick was so used to the magic that he didn't even notice it any more, and he never imagined it could be the key to a breakthrough. So instead, over the next few days, Patrick

tried every trick he could

find in a book Mum had bought to

help him form a connection with Oz. The book was called

Making the Top Dog.

"Socialization Is Vital" was the name of Chapter One.

Patrick looked up *socialization* and it meant *interacting*

with others. He really tried to encourage Oz to socialize,

but every time he attempted to lead his puppy from the

bedroom, Oz would give a sad whine that sounded so human that Patrick hadn't the heart to make the dog cross the threshold.

Patrick followed every step outlined in the book. He crawled on the floor like another dog. He spoke in a soft voice. He repeated Oz's name a hundred times a day. He shared hot dogs with Oz. He even shared doggie biscuits – which, truth be told, he found tasty – but nothing seemed to help. Oz would never come out of the crate unless Patrick was asleep. And then there was the issue of the trainer potty. Patrick assured Mum this was a good thing because it meant Oz was a smart puppy. Mum was not impressed, and Patrick started to worry that the summer holidays would end before he got through to Oz. And he hated to think of Oz shut up in his bedroom away from Dad and his allergies until Patrick got home from school each day.

One day Patrick sat cross-legged in front of Oz's crate. Boy and dog regarded each other with sad eyes.

"Come on, boy," said Patrick. "You have to come out. You need a bath and I'm running out of trainers. Please, Oz. I'm a nice guy. Honestly. You can trust me not to hurt you. How about I be your friend and you be mine? Then as a team we can go out and make more friends."

Oz's only reply was his trademark whine.

"OK, boy," sighed Patrick, and opened the next chapter of *Making the Top Dog*.

◆   ◆   ◆

Patrick's grandad walked into the room a bit later to see how the Oz project was going. He did this half a dozen times a day and always asked the same question: "Any progress, bud?"

"No," said Patrick gloomily. "And I only have one shoe left. After that, we're down to slippers."

Grandad squatted in front of Oz's box. "Hey, little fella. Don't you feel like coming out today?"

Oz whined again and Grandad froze.

"Hey!" he said, surprised.

"What?" asked Patrick.

Grandad squinted thoughtfully at Oz. "That dog has pretty good pitch."

"Very funny, Grandad," said Patrick.

"I'm not joking. I've been teaching Beethoven's "Ode to Joy" to a student downstairs all week. Apparently she's not the only one to have picked it up."

Patrick put down his book. "You're kidding?"

"Let's see," said Grandad, pulling a tin whistle from his pocket. It was his back-up instrument and more portable than the cello. He quickly played the theme. Oz looked at him from the back of his crate, then whined most of the notes back to him with a couple of extra ones at the end.

Grandad winked at his grandson. "As they say, bud: music soothes the savage beast. And it looks like it soothes the sad one, too."

Patrick stared at his puppy in total and utter amazement. "Oz!" he said. "You can sing?"

Grandad laughed. "Patrick, he's a dog. He can't sing. But he can whine pretty well."

Patrick felt an idea run through him like a jolt of electricity. His grandad might just have found the magical way to get Oz's bark back.

Patrick tugged his violin case from the high shelf where it had lain since Oz came into his life. Without Dad to dog him about practice, Patrick had neglected his instrument.

He tuned the strings, and as he tuned, Oz tuned his whine, matching Patrick as closely as his doggie vocal chords would allow.

"You have a great ear, Oz," said Patrick.

When he had finished tuning, Patrick played "Ode to Joy", which was a tune he knew too, and Oz howled it back at him. More or less.

Patrick tried the Darth Vader theme from *Star Wars* and Oz did that, too.

"Try this one, boy," said Patrick, and played a traditional Irish air called "Planxty Irwin". It took Oz a few listens with his head cocked to one side, but soon he had mastered it. This was incredible. Could his pup really be musical?

Oz's forepaws were now sticking out of the crate.

With every note, Patrick shifted a little bit away from the crate and Oz shifted with him, until, for the first time since arriving at his new home, Oz the rescue dog was all the way out of his crate while Patrick was awake.

Patrick smiled. "What do you say, Oz? Are we buddies at last?"

Oz's response was to piddle in a shoe by the window.

Patrick ran out to the landing and called down the stairs, "Grandad, the music is working. You're a genius!" Grandad's laughter echoed up the staircase, followed by the words: "It's about time everyone realized that, bud."

Patrick returned to his room wondering what tune to try on Oz next when he saw that another doggie problem had been solved.

Oz had found his new bed.

Patrick pulled out his phone and took a picture, which he sent to his dad in Australia.

Minutes later, his phone rang. His father's number flashed up on the screen.

Patrick swiped to answer. "Dad! Did you get the photo?"

"I did, Pat!" said his father's voice, which sounded clear even though he was in a different hemisphere. "I see you managed to get Oz out of his case and into another one!"

"Yep. I used the violin. Oz can sing, Dad."

Dad laughed. "I've been telling the boys in the band all about Oz. How you named him after our tour. They think it's hilarious. Keep sending the photos, son."

"I will. I took a good one of dog poo in my trainers. Do you want that?"

"Of course I do."

"Grandad said the composition was spectacular."

"Well, it must be true then."

Patrick took a deep breath. If Oz could be brave, he

could be brave. He looked at Oz asleep in the violin case and decided to ask some frank questions. "Don't you like Grandad any more, Dad? Is that why you're not coming to his house over the summer?"

Dad was silent for a moment, then he said, "No. I like your grandad lots. We have a few more gigs, that's all."

"I checked your website," said Patrick. "The last gig was a week ago."

"I know," said Dad. "But we have some private gigs. Last-minute stuff. Corporate. In Sydney."

Last-minute stuff often came in, and his dad always said: *In this game you can't turn down a paying job.*

"But you're not going to New Zealand?"

"Nope. Just Sydney."

"So when are you coming home? Exactly?"

"I'm not sure," said Dad. "We're still nailing down a few details."

"So, no date?"

"No date yet. Soon. And soon we'll have a proper talk."

"In person, Dad. Phone radiation is bad for my developing brain, you know?"

"I've heard that. I wouldn't want to interfere with your brain development."

"So – soon, Dad. You promise?"

"Soon," said Dad. "When I get things sorted."

But he didn't promise.

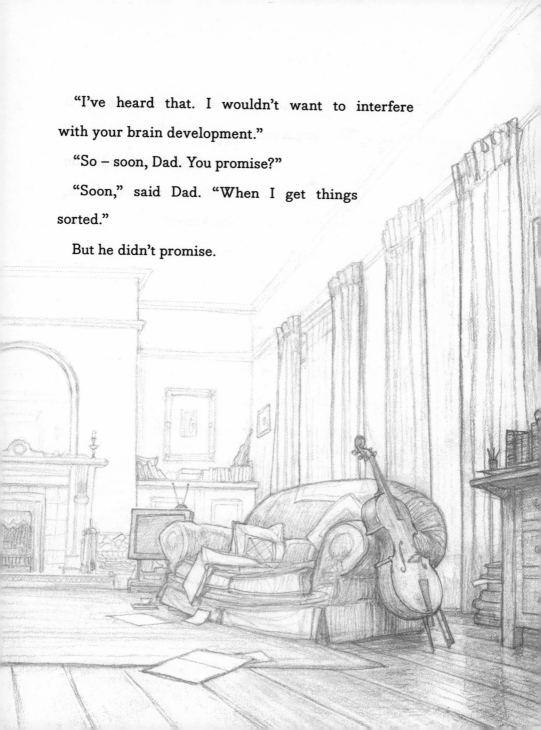

♦   ♦   ♦

Patrick told Mum about the conversation later when she was tucking him in, which she had started to do again this summer.

"Dad won't tell me when he's coming home," he said.

Mum sighed. "I can't help you there, Patrick. Dad will tell you when he's ready."

"There's something going on, isn't there?" said Patrick, but Mum changed the subject.

"I see Oz has found a new bed for himself. More comfortable than a crate, I bet."

"Grandad showed me how to get him out of the crate."

Mum pretended to be shocked. "*Grandad?* What about *me*? I bought you that book. Don't I deserve some credit?"

"Maybe twenty per cent," said Patrick.

"Only twenty?"

"Twenty for you, twenty for Grandad."

"Who gets the rest?" asked Mum, though she could guess.

"Oz," said Patrick. "Sixty per cent for Oz."

Chapter Six

After the initial breakthrough, things moved pretty quickly on the Oz front. Over the next few days, Patrick played the violin more than he had in a long while. He played jigs and reels. He played classical concertos and popular music. He played movie theme tunes and advertising jingles. In fact, he played everything he had learned in five years of lessons. And Oz howled or whined the notes back to him. (With the exception of country and western, which he didn't seem to care for.)

But progress stopped dead at a certain point.

Oz still would not leave the room. He howled any tune that Patrick would play and even composed a few of his own, which Grandad had to admit were pretty good. Oz would accept food from Patrick and he even allowed himself to be groomed, so long as Grandad played the cello downstairs while Patrick scrubbed him, and soon he was looking like a brand-new dog. His potty-training was going well insofar as Oz was happy to do his business on newspaper laid out in the corner of the bedroom, so Patrick was not forced to sacrifice his trainers any more. The violin case had become his permanent bed and he had begun to make a collection

of Patrick's old action figures in the lid; he used them as chew toys.

But no matter how hard Patrick tried to tempt him downstairs, Oz would stick no more than his nose outside the bedroom door. It seemed as though he was prepared to trust Patrick so far and no further.

Eventually, Patrick decided to give Zane a call. He explained the problem.

"I'm amazed you've got him out of the crate so quickly," said Zane. "But Oz is afraid to go outside because he still has no bark, buddy boy. He's howling but he isn't barking. You need to reach inside him and pull out his bark. (Not literally, of course, because your arm would get all slimy and Oz might bite your fingers off.) All I'm saying is: teach your dog to bark. Because when a dog barks at something, that dog isn't so afraid of that thing any more."

Zane made it sound easy. *Teach your dog to bark.* But how?

Patrick sat beside Oz with his violin across his knee and said firmly, "Come on, boy. Bark!"

But Oz just blinked and howled the opening bars of "Old MacDonald Had a Farm". Patrick checked the index of *Making the Top Dog* but there were no references to teaching a dog to bark. He called his friend Eric back at home, who had a Schnauzer also called Eric (which could be confusing), and Eric said, "I can't get my dog to *stop* barking. Do you want to trade dogs?"

Patrick answered that he did not.

Mum suggested that Patrick demonstrate to Oz how easy barking was, so Patrick knelt in front of Oz one afternoon feeling more than a little silly.

"Woof," he said. *"Woof woof. Arf arf."*

Oz looked at Patrick as though he might be a bit daft. And Patrick thought maybe Oz was right.

"Give Oz a fright," said Grandad. "Like you do when someone has hiccups."

But Patrick thought maybe Oz had already experienced enough frights in his life.

Patrick looked at doggie videos on YouTube and noticed that most dogs barked their heads off when there was a cat in the vicinity.

A cat! he thought. *I can pretend to be a cat.*

So one morning after a violin howling session, he sat in front of Oz and raised his hands like cat's paws. *"Miaow,"* he said. *"Miaow."*

Oz lifted his head and licked Patrick's fingers.

"Hey," said Patrick, laughing and pulling away his fingers. A lick was nice, but it wasn't a bark.

It was frustrating. Patrick spent every spare minute with Oz but still he couldn't get through. Oz seemed perfectly content to spend his time howling in Patrick's room.

"Don't you understand, boy?" Patrick asked him. "We

have to leave this room soon and go home."

But of course Oz didn't understand. He was a dog.

Mum had been busy teaching and thinking about Coin family life in general, but not too busy to notice that Patrick was missing his dad and their usual summer antics. And now his new dog was keeping them both cooped up inside.

If Patrick's father was here, she thought, the two of them would be outside playing right now.

And that thought led to another thought, which led to an idea.

Patrick was trying his latest make-Oz-bark idea when Mum knocked on his bedroom door.

"You're wearing a cat mask," she said as she entered the room.

"I made it myself," said Patrick. "I covered a balloon with papier mâché."

"Very realistic," said Mum.

Patrick took the mask off. "Oz doesn't seem to think so."

"Still no bark?"

"No bark," said Patrick glumly. "And we're no closer to going outside. Summer's halfway over and we haven't so much as played fetch."

Mum crossed the room to the window and drew back the net curtain.

"Well, maybe I can help you two guys out."

"I doubt it," said Patrick. "The entire internet couldn't help us out."

"Sometimes," said Mum, "mothers are wiser than the internet." And she opened the window, just a crack.

"Mum?" said Patrick. "What are you up to?"

Mum narrowed her eyes and waved her arms. "Magic, my doubting son," she said. "Magic."

For a moment, the magic had no effect on her doubting son, or his dog. Then Oz lifted his nose and sniffed.

ARF, said the dog.

Patrick was stunned. "Did you bark, boy? Was that a bark?"

ARF! ARF! barked Oz. There could be no doubt. Oz had his bark back.

Patrick could hardly believe it. He had a barking dog on his hands. "You did it, pal. You barked! You're a fully fledged barking dog."

"You see?" said Mum. "The wisdom of mothers must never be doubted."

"What did you do?" asked Patrick. "I tried everything."

Mum tapped her head. "I used the old noodle, Patrick. I said to myself, *Something is making that dog sad, just like something is making Patrick sad.*"

"I'm sad that Dad's so far away," said Patrick.

"Bingo," said Mum.

Before Patrick could figure this out, Oz had darted past him and stuck his nose out of the open window, barking for all he was worth. With each bark he kicked up his back legs and wagged his tail as if it was operated by a motor.

Patrick ran to the window and looked outside. Zane

stood on the pavement with a dog on a
lead. That dog looked like an older
version of Oz.

"Is that...?"

Mum nodded. "That's Oz's mother. Zane knew where to find her."

"Mum!" said Patrick. "You're unbelievable! A genius."

Mum curtsied. "Thank you, my son. You are absolutely right, of course."

Oz was so excited, he could hardly contain himself. He pranced around the room, lifting his paws high and barking like he was getting paid for it.

"Woohoo!" shouted Patrick, who felt like barking himself. "Go, Oz!"

But there were still hurdles to overcome before they could actually go out. A collar, for example. Whenever Patrick had tried to put a collar on Oz, the dog had retreated to his crate and stayed there for an hour. This time, Patrick put the collar on the floor in front of Oz's bed. The dog shrank away from it.

Mum opened the window even wider and Oz smelled his mother's scent.

ARF ARF ARF, said Oz to the collar. And whatever horrible memories he had stored in his doggie brain evaporated and the collar became simply a collar.

Patrick fastened the collar and clipped on a lead. Then Oz trotted behind Patrick as far as the stairway, where he pulled up short and whined the opening bars of Chopin's "Funeral March". This was not a good sign.

"Come on, Oz," said Patrick, starting down the stairs. "Come on, little fella. One step at a time."

ARF! said Oz, and he took the first step. It took a few more steps for him to become accustomed to stairs, but very soon dog and boy were on the ground floor. And the dog wasn't

finished yet. He needed to get outside and see his mother. He strained at the lead, pulling towards the front door.

It seemed that Oz was ready to venture outside. Patrick opened the front door and Oz stuck his nose into the sunshine, sniffed it, found it satisfactory and dragged Patrick outside onto the cracked city pavement, where his mother waited for him with licks and nuzzles.

"I love a family reunion," said Zane. "Your mum's a smart one. I should have thought of this myself."

"Oz is outside!" said Patrick. "I can't believe it."

Zane scratched Oz's head. "And he can visit any time.

I found her a home with Mrs Davidson at the end of the street. She just lost her old corgi. Oz's mother is perfect for her. I believe she's naming her Victoria."

Patrick knelt down and joined in the wriggling cuddle between Oz and his mother.

"I can't believe it," he said again. "I just can't believe you did it, Oz!"

Zane reached into his pocket and pulled out a tennis ball. "Hey, it's early yet. What do you say we walk on over to the park and play a little fetch?"

Patrick thought his head would explode. "Fetch? That would be amazing!" He turned to Mum and Grandad, who were standing at the door along with the other students and teachers, who had come out to see what all the commotion was about.

"Can I? Can I go?"

"Are you kidding, buddy?" said Grandad. "We're coming with you."

And they did. All of them. Patrick, Mum, Grandad, Zane, Oz, Victoria, three music teachers and eleven music students.

Chapter Seven

It was the best summer of Patrick's life. A summer that would have been absolutely perfect if Patrick's dad had been around to see it.

Patrick texted his dad every day and sent dozens of photos of Oz visiting his own mother, or getting up to various doggie antics such as chasing his own tail in the park or lying on his back in the sun with all paws raised and a look of utter bliss on his face. Dad always replied but would never offer any details on when he would be home to meet Oz in person, or indeed how he would manage that without sneezing his head off.

Mum was usually teaching, but she had Wednesdays and Sundays off so she dedicated those days to family outings. They made excursions to the beach, which Oz totally flipped over, spending hours tugging at sheaves of seaweed. They climbed to the top of Killiney Hill, which tired them all out. And they attended doggie parties where Oz got to hang out with some of the other dogs in the neighbourhood, including Victoria.

They had Oz thoroughly checked out by the local vet. All his vaccinations were brought up to date. His claws were clipped, his ears de-waxed and his coat trimmed.

All in all, by the middle of August, Oz had transformed from a traumatized, abandoned pup to a healthy, much-loved one.

And while Patrick was absorbed by his pal's transformation, he couldn't help noticing that sometimes when he looked at Mum and she wasn't expecting it, her face was sad.

Mum covered it well but Patrick didn't have to be a genius to realize the source of her sadness: Dad.

Chapter Eight

One afternoon Patrick tracked Mum to the garden hammock with the help of Oz's nose.

"Mum, I've been texting Dad for weeks now and he still won't say when he's coming home. What's going on?"

Mum sat up. "It's question time, is it? I'm surprised I escaped for this long."

"I have a whole lot of questions. Why are you sad, for one? And what's going to happen when we go home? I know you don't expect me to leave Oz with Grandad."

Oz heard his name and barked.

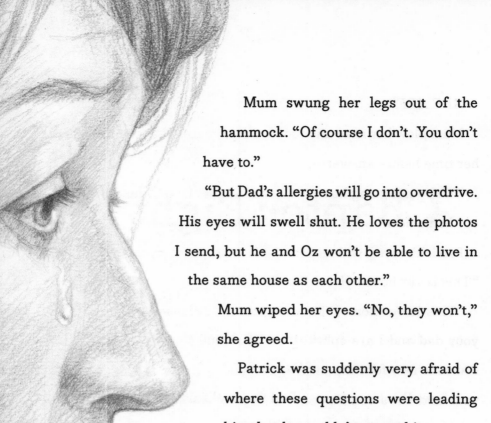

Mum swung her legs out of the hammock. "Of course I don't. You don't have to."

"But Dad's allergies will go into overdrive. His eyes will swell shut. He loves the photos I send, but he and Oz won't be able to live in the same house as each other."

Mum wiped her eyes. "No, they won't," she agreed.

Patrick was suddenly very afraid of where these questions were leading him, but he couldn't stop asking.

"Why are you crying? Is Dad sick? Is he dying?"

"No one's dying, Patrick," said Mum. "Calm down."

"Something's going on. You bought me off with Oz before..."

ARF ARF!

Mum blew her nose and took a deep breath. She took her time before answering.

"We're not going home, Pat," she said at last. "This is our home now."

Patrick's eyes widened and his mouth fell open. "This is our home? Here? Grandad's?"

"This is our home," Mum repeated. "Because your dad and I are splitting up. He found someone new for himself in Sydney last year and she's coming back with him. I don't want to be in the same village. So here we are."

Patrick couldn't believe it. *Dad was leaving them?* But Dad was Dad. His dad. Patrick had heard of other parents separating or getting divorced. But *his* parents?

"I talk to Dad every day and he never said

anything about someone new," said Patrick.

"No," said Mum. "He didn't. And he should have. I've told him a hundred times that it's not fair to keep you in the dark about this."

"But you and Dad love each other!"

"He doesn't love me any more," said Mum.

"But he loves *you*."

Patrick could not take in the information.

He had so many questions that they clogged up his throat like a blocked drain.

"But…" he said.

"And what if…?"

"Where are we supposed to…?"

Then he finally got a full one out. "Do you think it's for good?"

Mum nodded silently and Patrick simply froze, like a computer processing too many commands.

He stayed like that for a long time, then finally turned and walked back inside the house.

Oz whined and licked Mum's hand.

"Hey, boy," said Mum. "Don't worry. Patrick will be all right. Why don't I take you for a walk today?"

◆　◆　◆

Patrick lay on his bed and thought about his father. Patrick had always liked that his dad was a little different from other dads. He played the fiddle in a band, for one thing, and he had never been big on saying normal things like:

Make sure you get that toothbrush right in there at those back teeth. Or: *I know Geography is confusing, especially with all those tiny countries in Europe.* Instead, it seemed to Patrick that most of the things his father said to him were important, like: *Remember, son, there are things in the world that no one understands.* Or: *In the end, in almost every situation, it all boils down to quick thinking.* Or Patrick's favourite: *Most people you meet will be so stupid that they think they're smart, but a few will be smart*

enough to know they're stupid – and those are the clever
ones. Which made sense if you thought about it and was
also a joke and a tongue-twister, too.

And now Dad was not coming back.

Had he found a new son? A better one, who practised his
violin every day?

Patrick sent his dad a text. Have you found a better
son? Is that it?

Then, without even waiting for a reply, he switched

his phone off and threw it on the floor. He felt tricked by everyone. Dad had tricked him. Grandad had played along. Even Mum had distracted him with a dog.

Then Patrick realized something. Even if Dad changed his mind and wanted them to come home, they couldn't for as long as Oz was part of the package.

Patrick buried his face in the pillow and thought about this until his head hurt.

Grandad couldn't look after a dog. He didn't have five spare minutes in the week.

Whichever way Patrick looked at it, it was down to him to make this OK again.

Yes, Dad had left him. But it didn't have to stay like that. Situations could change. And one thing was sure – he wanted more than anything to have things back the way they were.

Then he made the toughest decision of his life. The idea made him sick to his stomach, but Patrick realized that Oz had to go.

His best friend had to go back to the shelter.

Chapter Nine

Oz knew that his new name was OZ because his buddy PATRICK said it a hundred times a day. And whenever PATRICK said his name now, Oz barked it right back at him: *OZ! OZ!*

It sounded a lot like regular barking, but Oz was pretty sure PATRICK could tell the difference because PATRICK was his best friend. Oz could also say *PAT-RICK*, which sounded a lot like regular barking too, but PATRICK knew. Oz was certain of it.

Oz was happier than he had been since he was taken

away from his mother, and to Oz happiness made the whole world actually brighter. The red velvet which lined his BED seemed to glow and his BOWL glinted silver in the light from the kitchen window.

Oz's bark was stronger than it had been since the BAD TIME, and there was nothing Oz liked better than to show off his bark. The first thing he did every day was to hop out of his special bed and patrol the house barking sharply in each room to warn any BAD THINGS that this house was under the protection of OZ THE TRUE DOG. And once this duty was completed and the HOME was safe, Oz would pick up his paws and trot across the kitchen tiles, which he did not fear any more even though they were red and white, and there he would find his buddy, the great PATRICK, kneeling over Oz's FOOD BOWL saying his name over and over. And each time the great PATRICK said it, Oz would bark the name right back at him.

But this morning PATRICK was not in the kitchen. Oz's

bowl was there with food in it, but it was not the right shape of food. PATRICK always poured the food in the shape of a little mountain with a peak in the middle. This food was smoothed off and flat.

Wrong, thought Oz, and did not eat the food.

The true and faithful Oz went in search of his buddy PATRICK and found him sitting in a chair in front of the PICTURE BOX. He did not react to Oz's hello bark. But he did react when Oz placed his head under PATRICK's dangling hand for a morning pat. His reaction was to get up and walk away without patting his buddy Oz.

So, no greeting and no pat.

Wrong. Wrong. WRONG.

Oz tried to follow PATRICK, but PATRICK pointed to the floor and made the sound "STAY", which Oz knew meant NO MOVING, so he did not move.

PATRICK climbed the stairs to his room and shut the door tight.

Oz was a little worried, but not too much.
PATRICK was GREAT AND AWESOME and would
be just fine once AWESOME PATRICK'S MUM
gave him a hug or maybe a drink of water.

But PATRICK was not *just fine* that day.
And, in fact, for many days afterwards it
seemed as though PATRICK had lost
that special PATRICK-ness that made
him GREAT AND AWESOME.

No matter how Oz barked or pranced, PATRICK did not want to play, and often the other good people would take Oz away from AWESOME PATRICK, as if his buddy did not want to see his friend.

And Oz would bark: *PAT-RICK! PAT-RICK! OZ!* to remind PATRICK that they were the best of friends.

Then a terrible thing happened and the mum took Oz in the car back to the MANY DOGS PLACE, which Oz remembered from the in-between times. In between BAD and GOOD. Where the person Zane was the boss.

Zane was good but not GOOD, and Oz spent the days away from PATRICK sitting quietly in his pen, remembering what it had been like when things were BAD. He would not play with the other dogs in his pen but kept his mind on PATRICK, wondering if he would ever see his friend again.

Oz was very afraid in his pen. He was afraid that there would be no more AWESOME SEAWEED and no more climbing green hills and no more WONDERFUL SOUNDS from Patrick's music stick and no more seeing his mother. He was so afraid that he did not eat the food Zane left for him.

Oz remembered how, after the bad times, PATRICK had come into his life and made him bark when he didn't want to in case the BAD PEOPLE hurt him. But now, because of PATRICK, he knew people could be AWESOME.

PATRICK had made him bark. Now he would make AWESOME PATRICK bark. He had to.

Chapter Ten

The only reason Mum had co-operated with Patrick's decision to send Oz back to the rescue shelter was because she thought the puppy's absence would make her son come to his senses. But after a week he was as stubborn as ever, so she decided that enough was enough.

Zane was at the desk when she arrived at the shelter to pick Oz up. "I was expecting to see you days ago," he said.

"I thought Patrick would crack," said Mum. "But he's got it into his head that his dad won't come back so long as Oz is around."

"He's hoping against hope, poor little man," said Zane. "Should I load him up?"

"Please," said Mum. "Patrick and that dog were meant to be together."

Zane went out the back, and moments later returned with Oz on his lead. "Look at that cute face," he said. "If anyone can bring Patrick back, it's this guy."

"I hope so," said Mum. "You can do it, can't you, boy?"

ARF, said Oz. *ARF ARF WOOF!*

Oz had waited with his nose pressed between the bars of his pen for Patrick to come. When the other dogs were yipping or eating or playing with their toys, Oz had stayed at his post waiting for AWESOME PATRICK.

PAT-RICK, he had thought. *PAT-RICK*. Over and over, the same thought, so that he could keep it in his head. The sun had gone up and down in the window seven times and then the door had opened and finally Oz smelled his friend. *PAT-RICK*, he barked. *PAT-RICK!*

But it was not AWESOME PATRICK. It was his mum, who had Patrick's scent on her clothes because of all the hugs they shared.

Oz whined a little, but at least PATRICK'S MUM was here. And maybe she would take Oz to PATRICK, which would be AWESOME.

The good people talked for a while and then Zane let Oz out of the pen and led him to the travel crate. Oz knew this meant he was going in the noisy machine and he jumped into the crate without hesitation, because the noisy machine usually went to PATRICK's house.

◆　　◆　　◆

In the Coin house, Patrick was looking at the TV but not really watching. He missed his dad and now he missed Oz, too. But he had to stay strong. It was Oz or Dad.

Those were the options.

That's stupid, said a voice in his head. *And you know it.*

Maybe it was stupid, but sometimes stupid things were true. Like, for instance, his own dad finding another family when he had one that loved him right here.

He turned on his phone and sent a quick text to his father: Sometimes stupid things are true.

And then he turned his phone off without glancing at the dozens of unread messages.

If Dad wanted to talk, he would have to do it face to face.

◆　　◆　　◆

Oz played it nice and quiet going in the front door, but once he caught a sniff of his buddy's scent, he was off like a bullet racing across the kitchen, his nails clicking on the tiles.

"Oz, come here, boy!" called Mum, but it was too late.

PAT-RICK! he barked. *PAT-RICK! OZ!*

PATRICK didn't react as Oz had hoped. Oz had been hoping for happy sounds like OZBUDDY! or C'MEREPAL. C'MEREPAL was one of his favourites because there was often wrestling after that. Oz thought that wrestling with

PATRICK was the most AWESOME thing in the world.

But there was no wrestling. PATRICK jumped a little when Oz barked, but instead of showing all his teeth in a big smile he hid his face behind his hands.

Oz kept barking but added in a tail-chase, spinning round and round till he felt dizzy and toppled over. Always a crowd-pleaser. But still PATRICK ignored him.

PAT-RICK! barked Oz. *PAT-RICK.*

Oz ran between PATRICK's legs and nuzzled his tummy, and while he was there, he smelled something.

A familiar smell from his days at the BAD PLACE. It was the smell of SADNESS, and Oz knew this because he used to smell like this himself until AWESOME PATRICK snapped him out of it. AWESOME PATRICK had made him lose the sad scent.

Oz yelped, because he'd had the doggie version of a brainwave. He pulled away from his buddy and ran upstairs.

"Oz!" Mum called. "You come down here. We've had enough drama and there are lessons going on."

Oz paid no attention, though he felt bad for ignoring AWESOME PATRICK's mother. He jumped on the bed and made an AWESOME BOUNCE onto the shelves, where he found what he needed.

The one thing that could bring PATRICK back to him.
The same thing that had brought him to AWESOME
PATRICK: the violin.

Oz took the instrument in his jaws, scrambled down-stairs and dropped the violin at Patrick's feet. The strings vibrated, sending a hum through the air.

"Oh, my..." said Mum. Patrick looked up.

Oz lifted his forepaw and tugged at the violin's strings, and Mum realized what this amazing, incredible dog was trying to do.

"That's it," she said. "Good boy!"

Oz twanged the strings again. And again. Sending up a flurry of notes that did not quite match each other but were music all the same. Then he barked.

Patrick blinked. "It's no use, Oz," he said crossly. "There's nothing I can do. I have no choice."

The dog played on, twanging with both paws, his tail wagging at the sound of Patrick's voice.

"Oz, stop," begged Patrick. "Mum. Please take Oz away."

But Mum was on the pup's side.

"Your bark," she said excitedly. "Oz is bringing back your bark! Good boy, Oz. Smart boy."

"He *is* smart," said Patrick. "I know. But how can we ever go home if I have a dog? It wouldn't be fair on Dad."

And this tipped Mum over into epic crack-up mode. Mum hadn't had an epic crack-up since she reversed the car into a bollard outside Tesco that time when she was late for Pilates. She had never had an epic crack-up at Patrick as far as he could remember. But now she was stamping her feet and waving her hands in the air.

"Fair on Dad?" she said. *"Fair on Dad?"*

"Dad has allergies," said Patrick quickly, sensing that

this had been the wrong thing to say.

"Allergies?" said Mum. *"Allergies,* is it? He's allergic to commitment. He's allergic to straight talking with his son. Oh, he has *allergies* all right."

Oz barked. This was EXCITING.

"Mum," said Patrick. "Dad will come back."

Mum laughed. "Oh, he'll come back. Of course he will. For ten minutes or maybe an hour and then he'll swan off back to his new girlfriend. Heaven forbid he might sneeze while he's here, right, Patrick? That would be awful."

Patrick was a little shocked to hear Mum talk about Dad in this way. There was a moment's silence. Then he said in a small voice, "Mum. Do you hate Dad now?"

"No, sweetie," said Mum. "I don't hate your father. I'm just very cross with him right now. And he loves you as much as he ever did. But you need to understand, Patrick, that things are different now." Mum sat on the arm of the chair and hugged Patrick. "We have a tough year ahead of us, Pat. Getting used to this new life. You'll have to go to a new school and make new friends. Grandad has to get used to us living here. I have to go back to work full-time. We need all the friends we can get. You have a friend, Patrick. You have the best friend a boy could ever have. And he loves you even when it looks like you don't love him any more."

And all of a sudden Mum began to cry. The tears gushed out of her in waves and her entire body shook. She collapsed onto Patrick's shoulder and he patted her awkwardly on the back.

Oz was a smart dog and knew an opportunity when he saw one.

He clambered onto the chair, wiggling his furry body between Patrick and his mum. He licked Patrick's face and Patrick knew that he had been stupid to send his dog away.

"I'm sorry, boy," he said. "Pals for ever, OK? Can you forgive me?"

Mum wailed. "Of course he'll forgive you, dopey. He's a dog."

They cried together for a few minutes, and Oz howled the theme from James Bond, which was one of his favourites.

Grandad stuck his head in the door.

"What's going on here?" he asked. "The end of the world? Some of us are trying to work, you know."

Mum had just downgraded from a bawl to a sniffle, but seeing her father set her off again.

"I can spare five seconds for a hug," said Grandad. "I have a student in the next room."

As it turned out, Grandad stayed in the hug for almost three full minutes before climbing off the chair.

"We're keeping Oz, then, I take it?" he said.

"If that's OK," said Patrick, looking down at his feet.

"Of course it's OK. Everyone loves Oz. I think students have started to sign up just to hear the amazing singing dog. But what about when your dad comes to visit?"

Patrick thought about this. "Maybe Mum would take Oz for a walk while he's here."

"Or," said Mum, "your dad could take an antihistamine. Imagine that. He'd have to take a tiny pill every single time. The horror." Then she said, "Sorry. That's a new personality trait I'm developing. Sarcasm. I'm sorry, Patrick."

PAT-RICK, barked Oz. *PAT-RICK.*

"You know, Mum," said Patrick, "I think that when Oz barks, he's trying to say Patrick. You know: PAT-RICK."

PAT-RICK, said Oz.

Mum hugged the boy and his dog tightly. "I think Oz is a very clever dog."

Both of the humans were correct.

"Now," said Mum. "We need to start sorting things out. Do you think you're ready to talk to your father? I know you haven't been replying to his texts."

"We need to talk, not text," said Patrick firmly. Patrick's phone was on the coffee table. Mum picked it up and passed it over.

"You need to tell your father that, sweetie," she said.

Patrick took the phone and scrolled to Dad's number.

PAT-RICK! said Oz. *PAT-RICK! PAT-RICK.*

And while he waited for his dad to answer, Patrick wrapped his free arm around his best friend's neck.

◆　　◆　　◆

Oz felt PATRICK's fingers in his fur and he knew that everything was AWESOME again. There would be GOOD people and green hills and wonderful food. He would HOWL along with Patrick's music stick. He would go and see Mother and she would tell him stories.

And in the evening he would sleep in his red velvet bed.

Oz was a clever dog and he knew that sometimes BAD THINGS would happen. But bad things were no match for GOOD DOG OZ and AWESOME PATRICK. They would be together for ever.

My boy, thought Oz. *AWESOME PATRICK will always be MY BOY.*